Geronimo Stilton
ENGLISH!

23 MY CITY 我居住的城市

U0061304

新雅文化事業有限公司
www.sunya.com.hk

Geronimo Stilton English
MY CITY　我居住的城市

作　　者：Geronimo Stilton 謝利連摩·史提頓
譯　　者：申倩
責任編輯：王燕參
封面繪圖：Giuseppe Facciotto
插圖繪畫：Claudio Cernuschi, Andrea Denegri, Daria Cerchi
內文設計：Angela Ficarelli, Raffaella Picozzi
出　　版：新雅文化事業有限公司
　　　　　香港英皇道499號北角工業大廈18樓
　　　　　電話：（852）2138 7998
　　　　　傳真：（852）2597 4003
　　　　　網址：http://www.sunya.com.hk
　　　　　電郵：marketing@sunya.com.hk
發　　行：香港聯合書刊物流有限公司
　　　　　香港新界大埔汀麗路36號中華商務印刷大廈3字樓
　　　　　電話：（852）2150 2100　傳真：（852）2407 3062
　　　　　電郵：info@suplogistics.com.hk
印　　刷：C & C Offset Printing Co.,Ltd
　　　　　香港新界大埔汀麗路36號
版　　次：二〇一二年七月初版
　　　　　10 9 8 7 6 5 4 3 2 1

版權所有·不准翻印
中文繁體字版權由 Atlantyca S.p.A. 授予
Original title: LA MIA CITTÀ
Based upon an original idea by Elisabetta Dami
www.geronimostilton.com

Geronimo Stilton names, characters and related indicia are copyright, trademark and exclusive license of Atlantyca
S.p.A. All Rights Reseved.
The moral right of the author has been asserted.

Stilton is the name of a famous English cheese. It is a registered trademark of the Stilton Cheese Makers' Association.
For more information go to www.stiltoncheese.com

No part of this book may be stored, reproduced or transmitted in any form or by any means, electronic or mechanical,
including photocopying, recording, or by any information storage and retrieval system, without written permission
from the copyright holder. For information address Atlantyca S.p.A., via Leopardi 8 - 20123 Milan, Italy -
foreignrights@atlantyca.it - www.atlantyca.com

ISBN: 978-962-08-5552-8
© 2008 Edizioni Piemme S.p.A., Via Tiziano 32 - 20145 Milano - Italia
International Rights © 2007 Atlantyca S.p.A. - via Leopardi, 8, Milano - Italy
© 2012 for this Work in Traditional Chinese language, Sun Ya Publications (HK) Ltd.
18/F, North Point Industrial Building, 499 King's Road, Hong Kong.
Published and printed in Hong Kong

CONTENTS
目錄

BENJAMIN'S CLASSMATES
班哲文的老師和同學們

Maestra Topitilla
托比蒂拉・德・托比莉斯

Rarin
拉琳

Diego
迪哥

Rupa
露芭

Tui
杜爾

David
大衛

Sakura
櫻花

Mohamed
穆哈麥德

Tian Kai
田凱

Oliver
奧利佛

Milenko
米蘭哥

Trippo
特里普

Carmen
卡敏

Atina
阿提娜

Esmeralda
愛絲梅拉達

Pandora
潘朵拉

Takeshi
北野

Kuti
菊花

Benjamin
班哲文

Hsing
阿星

Laura
羅拉

Kiku
奇哥

Antonia
安東妮婭

Liza
麗莎

GERONIMO AND HIS FRIENDS
謝利連摩和他的家鼠朋友們

謝利連摩・史提頓 Geronimo Stilton
一個古怪的傢伙，簡直可以說是一隻笨拙的文化鼠。他是
《鼠民公報》的總裁，正花盡心思改變報紙業的歷史。

菲・史提頓 Tea Stilton
謝利連摩的妹妹，她是《鼠民公報》的特派記者，同
時也是一個運動愛好者。

班哲文・史提頓 Benjamin Stilton
謝利連摩的小侄兒，常被叔叔稱作「我的
小乳酪」，是一隻感情豐富的小老鼠。

潘朵拉・華之鼠 Pandora Woz
柏蒂・活力鼠的姨甥女、班哲文最好的朋友，
是一隻活潑開朗的小老鼠。

柏蒂・活力鼠 Patty Spring
美麗迷人的電視新聞工作者，致力於她熱愛的電視事業。

賴皮 Trappola
謝利連摩的表弟，非常喜歡食物，風趣幽默，是一隻饞
嘴、愛開玩笑的老鼠，善於將歡樂傳遞給每一隻鼠。

麗萍姑媽 Zia Lippa
謝利連摩的姑媽，對鼠十分友善，又和藹可親，只想將
最好的給身邊的鼠。

艾拿 Iena
謝利連摩的好朋友，充滿活力，熱愛各項運動，他希望
能把對運動的熱誠傳給謝利連摩。

史童克・愛管閒事鼠 Ficcanaso Squitt
謝利連摩的好朋友，是一個非常有頭腦的私家
偵探，總是穿着一件黃色的乾濕褸。

A GUIDEBOOK OF TOPAZIA
妙鼠城旅遊指南

親愛的小朋友，歡迎來到妙鼠城！我正在編寫一本關於妙鼠城的旅遊指南。首先我要遊覽一下整座城市，班哲文和潘朵拉想陪我一起遊覽，你們也一起來吧。我以一千塊莫澤雷勒乳酪發誓，我會帶你們好好遊覽老鼠島迷人的首都——妙鼠城的！一想到這裏，我的鬍子就激動得顫抖起來！妙鼠城裏有很多東西等着我們去發掘，很多新詞彙等着我們去學習呢，當然是英語啦！

I've got to write a guidebook of Topazia...

... and I'm going to go on a city tour!

We could help you.

Can we come with you, Uncle Geronimo?

We could help you.
我們可以幫助你。

在英文中，town指市鎮，city指城市。一般來説，市鎮比城市小。

跟我謝利連摩·史提頓一起學英文，就像玩遊戲一樣簡單好玩！

你可以一邊看着圖畫一邊讀。
以下有幾個標誌，你要特別留意：

當看到 🔘 標誌時，你可以聽CD，一邊聽，一邊跟着朗讀，還可以跟着一起唱歌。

當看到 ⭐ 標誌時，你可以和朋友們一起玩遊戲，或者嘗試回答問題。題目很簡單，它們對鞏固你所學過的內容很有幫助。

當看到 ❗ 標誌時，你要注意看一下格子裏的生字，反覆唸幾遍，掌握發音。

最後，不要忘記完成小測驗和練習冊裏的問題！看看你有多聰明吧。

祝大家學得開開心心！

謝利連摩·史提頓

BUY THE TICKET　買車票

我們來到會唱歌的石頭廣場 (Pietra Che Canta Square)，在那裏等候旅遊巴。班哲文和潘朵拉興奮得連皮毛也豎起來了，這是多麼美妙的一趟旅行啊！看，旅遊巴來了，我們可以上車了！第一件要做的事當然是買車票啦。

buy the ticket
買車票

Benjamin buys his ticket too and goes looking for a seat.

8

A SONG FOR YOU!

 Track 1

The Wheels on the Bus

The wheels on the bus go
round and round,
round and round, round and round.
The wheels on the bus go
round and round,
all through the town.

The doors on the bus go
open and shut,
open and shut, open and shut.
The doors on the bus go
open and shut,
all through the town.

The wipers on the bus go
swish, swish, swish!
Swish, swish, swish!
Swish, swish, swish!
The wipers on the bus go
swish, swish, swish!
All through the town.

The horn on the bus goes
beep, beep, beep!
Beep, beep, beep! Beep, beep, beep!
The horn on the bus goes
beep, beep, beep!
All through the town.

The money on the bus goes
clink, clink, clink!
Clink, clink, clink! Clink, clink, clink!
The money on the bus goes clink, clink, clink!
All through the town.

The gas on the bus goes
glug, glug, glug!
Glug, glug, glug!
Glug, glug, glug!
The gas on the bus goes
glug, glug, glug!
All through the town.

The driver on the bus says:
'Move on back, move on back,
move on back!'
The driver on the bus says:
'Move on back!'
All through the town.

The baby on the bus says
'Wah, wah, wah!
Wah, wah, wah! Wah, wah, wah!'
The baby on the bus says
'Wah, wah, wah!'
All through the town.

The people on the bus say:
'Shh, shh, shh, shh, shh, shh,
shh, shh, shh!'
The people on the bus say: 'Shh, shh, shh!'
All through the town.

The bell on the bus goes ting-a-ling-a-ling!
Ting-a-ling-a-ling! Ting-a-ling-a-ling!
The bell on the bus goes ting-a-ling-a-ling!

Stop! This bus is too
crowded! I want to get off!

9

TURN RIGHT... GO LEFT...
向右轉……向左走……

妙鼠城之旅開始了。導遊一路上給大家
介紹行程，我以一千塊莫澤雷勒乳酪發誓，
妙鼠城的景點真多啊！

We are going to see the most famous monuments in Topazia!

1

We'll go straight down Leonardo da Sguinci Road...

2

... then we'll go round the arch.

3

We'll take Lgattidilà Street...

4

railway station

... and, finally, we'll go down Lgattidiquà Street until we get to the railway station.

Let's look at the route on the map!

Yes, it's fun!

10

第一站是妙鼠城火車站，這裏非常熱鬧，每天從這裏出發和到達這裏的市民很多，運載乘客和貨物的火車來往不絕……

Many trains leave and arrive at Topazia railway station.

go straight down 沿着……直走
go round 繞着……走
go down 沿着……走

In front of the railway station there's the bus terminal.

Behind the railway station there's a big car park.

ON THE BUS 在巴士上

接着，我們來到了港口區。我以一千塊莫澤雷勒乳酪發誓，這裏的風景真美麗！導遊沿途給大家介紹很多著名的建築物，有妙鼠城運動場、體育中心等。你也跟着一起學習用英語說說看吧。

The bus continues along Quandoilgattononcè Street.

It reaches the crossroads with Robiola Street and turns left into Mascarpone Street.

It goes into Lapallainbuca Square where the stadium is.

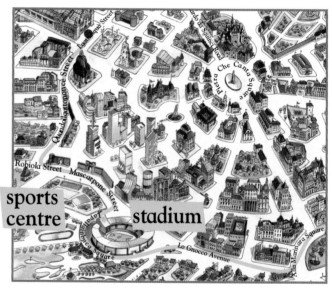

It goes down Lo Gnocco Avenue and stops at the Alla Marinara Square bus stop.

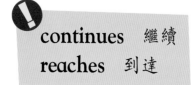

continues　繼續
reaches　到達

12

You can see the sports centre on your right!

Yes, we always come here with Aunt Patty!

Did you see the stadium on your left?

Yes, we came here together to see a match!

The funfair's big wheel!

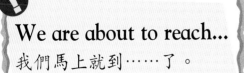

Now, look out of the window: what can you see on your right?

We are about to reach the harbour where we'll stop and have a break.

A TRAFFIC JAM　交通擠塞

　　在前往妙鼠城河的路上，我們不幸遇上了大塞車！導遊和司機正在討論走哪條路線最好。我知道有一條捷徑，是我妹妹菲告訴我的，我馬上通知導遊和司機。於是我們走了一條新的路線，很快就到達目的地了！

Driver: There is a traffic jam, I have to take a different road to get to the river.
Guide: Leave Del Polpo Square and turn right.

Ger: Oh, no! You're going the wrong way! You need to turn left, take Sorciodimare Avenue and continue into Stella Marina Street.

Guide: You're right, Mr. Stilton! I'll turn left at the end of Stella Marina Street, then I'll take the first street on the right.

Ger: You can't! It's a one-way street. You have to take the second on the right!

Turn right!
向右轉
Turn left!
向左轉

one-way street
單程路

sports centre

stadium

funfair

WHERE WOULD YOU LIKE TO GO? 你想去哪裏？

　　旅遊巴在河邊停下來，這時柏蒂開着吉普車剛好趕上我們。班哲文和潘朵拉提議大家一起坐上柏蒂的車子，沿着河邊繼續遊覽……我以一千塊莫澤雷勒乳酪發誓，這真是美好的一天！

Where would you like to go, kids?

Let's go and see the Toma Mountains!

It's too late to go out of town!

Ok, let's go on a trip along the riverside then!

Why don't we stop now and have a break?

Ok, on the other side of the river there's a panoramic view.

 試着用英語説出：「你想去哪裏？」

答案：Where would you like to go?

16

這天我們都玩得很開心，可是柏蒂的吉普車顛簸得太厲害，使我覺得有點暈車。所以我們還是選擇坐地鐵回家！

A SONG FOR YOU!

Track 2

Turn Left, Turn Right

Turn left, go straight ahead
up to the square,
then turn right.
Take the first street
on the left,
and the second street
on the right!

And now my dear friend
listen to what I say:
if you didn't get lost,
you must be right there!

ON THE MASS TRANSIT RAILWAY (MTR) 在地鐵上

柏蒂載我們去了地鐵站，很快我們便可以回到家了……地鐵站裏的設施真多啊，班哲文和潘朵拉很開心，因為他們又有機會學習新的英文詞彙了。

MTR	地鐵
MTR station	地鐵站
coach	車廂
train	列車
escalator	扶手電梯
lift	升降機
platform	月台
concourse	大堂

Shall we use the escalator?
我們可以乘扶手電梯嗎？

BACK HOME　回到家裏

今天過得真愉快……但驚喜還沒結束呢！瑪嘉蓮姑媽到我家來了，她還準備了美味的蛋糕呢！班哲文和潘朵拉想不出有什麼事情比吃到瑪嘉蓮姑媽做的芝士蛋糕更讓人高興的了……瑪嘉蓮姑媽真是一位烹飪高手！

〈在城市下面〉

班哲文：那些警察為什麼要我們幫忙？

謝利連摩：我不知道，但很快他們就會告訴我們。

史奎克：但是他們要我們保守秘密。

警察：你們有沒有聽聞過關於妙鼠城女王的珠寶的事呀？

謝利連摩：有呀，它們被偷走了，至今還沒找到。

史奎克：但我是一位偵探，我一定會找到它們的。

警察：其實我們已經找到它們了。

警察：但是……我女兒以為那些珠寶是玩具，她把它們戴在身上，丟失了。

謝利連摩：在哪裏丟失的？

掉進水槽裏，結果被沖到妙鼠城的溝渠裏。

班哲文：所以我們必須下去溝渠裏去找。

賴皮：謝利連摩，你可以給我們指路嗎？

謝利連摩：我——我——我？！

賴皮：謝利連摩，你怕黑嗎？

謝利連摩：不——不——不……但燈在哪裏？

班哲文：來吧，我先走了！

謝利連摩：我要回去了……我需要一些新鮮空氣！

班哲文：等等……看！

菲：太好了，班哲文！你找到那些珠寶了！

賴皮：我們現在出去吧！

潘朵拉：小心呀！

謝利連摩：哎呀！

班哲文：叔叔，你沒事吧？

謝利連摩：我沒事，但我的衣服髒透了！

第二天……

班哲文：你今天看過報紙了嗎？

謝利連摩：還沒看。你為什麼這樣問？

謝利連摩：馬上離開這裏吧！快點！

潘朵拉：外面是什麼聲音呢？

〔一把聲音說〕我們的英雄們在這裏！

謝利連摩：什麼？

班哲文：報紙上說你找到了那些珠寶，但你……需要洗一個澡！

謝利連摩：啊！

TEST 小測驗

⭐ 1. 用英語說出下面的詞彙。

(a) 巴士　　　**(b)** 座位　　　**(c)** 車票

⭐ 2. 潘朵拉和班哲文在說什麼?讀出他們的對話,並用中文說出句子的意思。

(a)

Let's look at the route on the map!

Yes, it's fun!

(b)

I want to sit near the window.

Ok, I'm sitting next to you.

⭐ 3. 用英語說出下面的詞彙。

(a) 市鎮　　**(b)** 城市　　**(c)** 街道　　**(d)** 廣場　　**(e)** 大街　　**(f)** 道路

⭐ 4. 用英語說出下面的句子。

(a) 你在你的左面能看到什麼?
What can ... ... ?

(b) 你在你的右面能看到什麼?
What can ... ... ?

(c) 向左轉!
... ... !

(d) 向右轉!
... ... !

24

DICTIONARY 詞典

（英、粵、普發聲）

A

air　空氣

arrive　到達

avenue　大街

B

behind　後面

bridges　橋

bus　巴士

bus stop　巴士站

bus terminal　巴士總站

buy　買

C

car park　停車場

city　城市

clean　乾淨

clink　叮噹聲

clothes　衣服

coach　車廂

concourse　大堂

continues　繼續

crossroads　十字路口

crowded　擠擁的（普：擁擠的）

D

daughter　女兒

detective 偵探

doors 門

driver 司機

go straight down
沿着……直走

guide 導遊

guidebook 旅遊指南

E

escalator 扶手電梯

F

famous 著名的

fast 快

finally 最後

first 第一

fresh 新鮮

G

glug 咕嚕咕嚕聲

go down 沿着……走

go round 繞着……走

H

harbour 港口

have a break 休息

help 幫助

heroes 英雄

horn 警笛

I

in front of 前面

J

jewels 珠寶

L

leave 離開

lift 升降機

M

map 地圖

match 比賽

monuments 歷史遺跡

mountains 山

MTR 地鐵

MTR station 地鐵站

N

near 近

newspaper 報紙

O

oldest 最古老的

on the other side 另一邊

on your left 在你的左面

on your right 在你的右面

one-way street 單程路

open 開

outside 外面

over there 在那裏

P

panoramic view 全景

photo 照片

platform 月台

police 警察

Q

queen 女王

R

railway station 火車站

reaches 到達

river 河

riverside 河邊

road 道路

route 路線

S

seat　座位

second　第二

sewers　溝渠

shut　關上

sink　水槽

smallest　最小的

sports centre　體育中心

square　廣場

stadium　運動場

street　街道

surprise　驚喜

swish　嗖嗖聲

T

third　第三

ticket　車票

tour　旅遊

town　市鎮

traffic jam　交通擠塞
　（普：交通堵塞）

train　列車

turn left　向左轉

turn right　向右轉

W

watch out　小心

wheels　車輪

window　窗子

wipers　雨刷

wrong　錯誤

看在一千塊莫澤雷勒乳酪的份上，你學得開心嗎？很開心，對不對？好極了！跟你一起跳舞唱歌我也很開心！我等着你下次繼續跟班哲文和潘朵拉一起玩一起學英語呀。現在要說再見了，當然是用英語說啦！

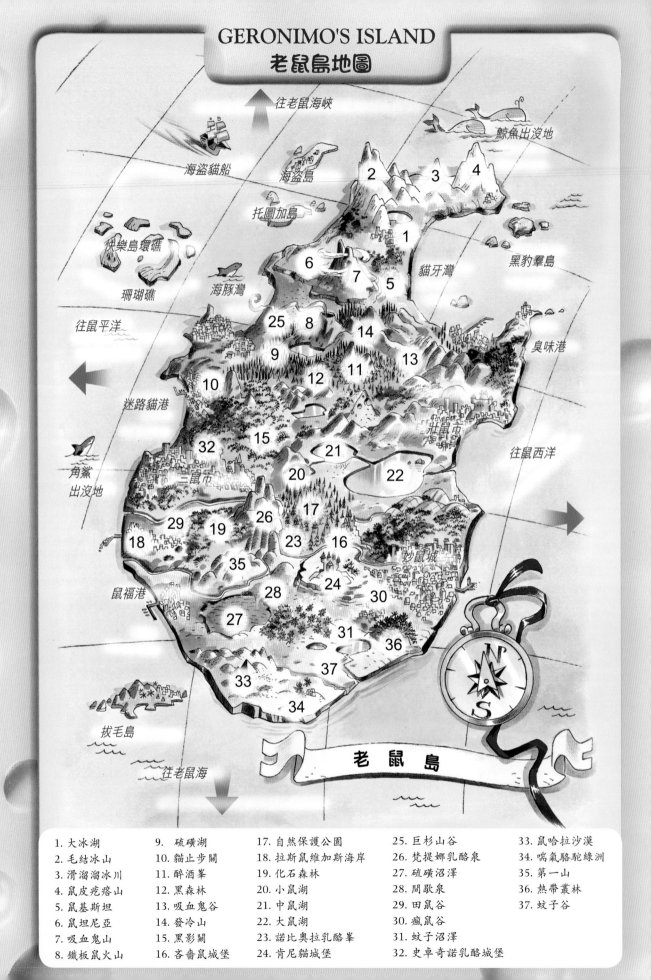

GERONIMO'S ISLAND
老鼠島地圖

往老鼠海峽

鯨魚出沒地

海盜貓船

海盜島

托圖加島

貓牙灣

黑豹羣島

快樂島環礁

珊瑚礁　海豚灣

往鼠平洋

臭味港

往鼠西洋

迷路貓港

壯鼠市

角鯊
出沒地

三鼠市

妙鼠城

鼠福港

老鼠島

拔毛島

往老鼠海

1. 大冰湖	9. 硫磺湖	17. 自然保護公園	25. 巨杉山谷	33. 鼠哈拉沙漠
2. 毛結冰山	10. 貓止步關	18. 拉斯鼠維加斯海岸	26. 梵提娜乳酪泉	34. 喘氣駱駝綠洲
3. 滑溜溜冰川	11. 醉酒峯	19. 化石森林	27. 硫磺沼澤	35. 第一山
4. 鼠皮疙瘩山	12. 黑森林	20. 小鼠湖	28. 間歇泉	36. 熱帶叢林
5. 鼠基斯坦	13. 吸血鬼谷	21. 中鼠湖	29. 田鼠谷	37. 蚊子谷
6. 鼠坦尼亞	14. 發冷山	22. 大鼠湖	30. 瘋鼠谷	
7. 吸血鬼山	15. 黑影關	23. 諾比奧拉乳酪峯	31. 蚊子沼澤	
8. 鐵板鼠火山	16. 客嗇鼠城堡	24. 肯尼貓城堡	32. 史卓奇諾乳酪城堡	

Geronimo Stilton

EXERCISE BOOK

練習冊

想知道自己對 MY CITY 掌握了多少，
趕快打開後面的練習完成它吧！

ENGLISH!

23 **MY CITY** 我居住的城市

A GUIDEBOOK OF TOPAZIA
妙鼠城旅遊指南

⭐ 謝利連摩想編寫一本關於妙鼠城的旅遊指南，看看他們在說什麼，從下面選出適當的字詞填在橫線上，完成他們的對話吧。

help	city tour	come
write	guidebook	

1. I've got to _____ a _____ of Topazia...

2. ... and I'm going to go on a _____ .

3. We could _____ you.

4. Can we _____ with you, Uncle Geronimo?

FIND THE RIGHT WORDS!
字詞配對

⭐ 讀出下面的英文詞彙，然後找出相應的中文詞彙，把代表答案的英文字母填在空格裏。

1. river ☐

2. railway station ☐

3. square ☐

4. road ☐

5. riverside ☐

6. town ☐

7. bus ☐

8. crossroads ☐

9. stadium ☐

10. sports centre ☐

11. bridges ☐

A. 體育中心

B. 運動場

C. 巴士

D. 橋

E. 河

F. 火車站

G. 河邊

H. 道路

I. 市鎮

J. 廣場

K. 十字路口

MY TICKET, YOUR TICKET...
我的車票，你的車票……

★ 這是誰的車票？從下面選出適當的字詞填在橫線上，完成他們的對話。

our	my	your	their

1.

This is _____ ticket.

2.

This is _____ ticket.

3.

These are _____ tickets.

These are _____ tickets.

4.

3

TURN RIGHT... GO LEFT...
向右轉……向左走……

⭐ 謝利連摩和孩子們乘着旅遊巴出發了。想知道他們去過妙鼠城哪些地方？從下面選出適當的字詞填在橫線上，完成句子，就知道了。

round	down	railway station	until	take

1. We'll go straight _____ Leonardo da Sguinci Road.

2. Then, we'll go _____ the arch.

3. We'll _____ Lgattidilà Street.

4. Finally, we'll go down Lgattidiquà Street _____ we get to the _____ .

AT THE RAILWAY STATION
在火車站裏

⭐ 根據圖畫，從下面選出適當的字詞填在橫線上，完成短文。

car park   bus terminal   railway station

Many trains leave and arrive at Topazia

1. _____ . Behind the railway station

there's a big 2. _____ .

In front of the railway station

there's the 3. _____ .

A TRAFFIC JAM 交通擠塞

⭐ 根據圖畫，從下面選出適當的字詞填在橫線上，完成句子。

one-way	left	way	jam

There is a traffic _____!
Turn right!

Oh, no! You're going the wrong _____!
You need to turn left!

I'll turn _____, then I'll take the first street on the right.

You can't! It's a _____ street.
You have to take the second on the right!

ON THE MASS TRANSIT RAILWAY 在地鐵上

⭐ 謝利連摩和孩子們準備乘地鐵回家。地鐵站裏的設施真多,把下面的英文字母重新排列好,然後在橫線上寫出來,你就知道地鐵站裏有些什麼設施了。

1. hoacc _____

2. nirat _____

3. afptlmor _____

4. onrcucoes _____

5. iltf _____

6. rtesalcao _____

ANSWERS 答案

TEST 小測驗

1. (a) bus   (b) seat   (c) ticket

2. (a) 潘朵拉：我們來看看地圖上的路線吧！
      班哲文：好，這真有趣！
  (b) 潘朵拉：我想坐在靠窗的位置。
      班哲文：好的，我就坐在你的旁邊吧。

3. (a) town   (b) city   (c) street   (d) square   (e) avenue   (f) road

4. (a) What can <u>you see on your left</u>?   (b) What can <u>you see on your right</u>?
  (c) <u>Turn left</u>!   (d) <u>Turn right</u>!

EXERCISE BOOK 練習冊

P.1
1. write, guidebook   2. city tour   3. help   4. come

P.2
1. E   2. F   3. J   4. H   5. G   6. I
7. C   8. K   9. B   10. A   11. D

P.3
1. my   2. your   3. our   4. their

P.4
1. down   2. round   3. take   4. until, railway station

P.5
1. railway station   2. car park   3. bus terminal

P.6
1. jam   2. way   3. left   4. one-way

P.7
1. coach   2. train   3. platform   4. concourse   5. lift   6. escalator